OUR FUTURE IN SPACE

SPACE WORKERS

MAKING MONEY ABOVE EARTH

David Jefferis

Crabtree Publishing Company

www.crabtreebooks.com

INTRODUCTION

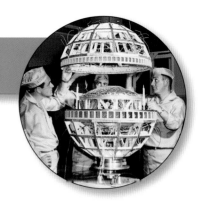

Can space workers really make money? Well, the answer is a big yes. Space **commerce** is a huge business, with thousands of companies earning billions of dollars. They may launch rockets, make **artificial satellites** and sell the information they supply, or build ground stations.

Satellites provide **data** for TV, radio, navigation, photos, and videos. But the future holds more than information only. In years to come, there could be mining on the Moon or searching deep in space for valuable resources. Read on to learn more!

↑ Technicians prepare an early TV satellite for launch in 1962. Since then, thousands of satellites have been launched into space.

🌳 Crabtree Publishing Company

www.crabtreebooks.com   1-800-387-7650

Written and produced for Crabtree Publishing by:
David Jefferis

Technical advisor:
Mat Irvine FBIS (Fellow of the British Interplanetary Society)

Editors:
Mat Irvine, Janine Deschenes

Prepress Technicians:
Mat Irvine, Ken Wright

Proofreader:
Petrice Custance

Print Coordinator:
Margaret Amy Salter

Acknowledgements
We wish to thank all those people who have helped to create this publication and provided images.
Individuals:
    David Ducross/ESA
    Vaughan Ling
    David Jefferis
    Gavin Page
    Luca Oleastri/Fotolia
Organizations:
    Arianespace
    Blue Origin
    Boeing Corp
    Canadian Space Agency
    DSI Deep Space Industries

ESA European Space Agency
Google
H3 Corporation
JPL Jet Propulsion Laboratory
Lionsgate films
Lockheed Martin
Made in Space Inc
Microsatellite Systems
    Canada Inc
NASA Space Agency
NASDA, JAXA, Japanese
    Space Agencies
Reaction Engines Ltd
Shackleton Energy
SpaceX
US Air Force

The right of David Jefferis to be identified as the Author of this work has been asserted by him in accordance with the Copyrights, Designs and Patents Act 1988.

Printed in the USA/102017/CG20170907

Library and Archives Canada Cataloguing in Publication

Jefferis, David, author
        Space workers / David Jefferis.

(Our future in space)
Includes index.
Issued in print and electronic formats.
ISBN 978-0-7787-3537-3 (hardcover).--
ISBN 978-0-7787-3549-6 (softcover).--
ISBN 978-1-4271-1943-8 (HTML)

        1. Space industrialization--Juvenile literature. 2. Outer space--Civilian use--Juvenile literature. I. Title.

HD9711.75.J44 2017   j338.0919   C2017-905190-3
                                                                        C2017-905191-1

Library of Congress Cataloging-in-Publication Data

CIP available at the Library of Congress

CONTENTS

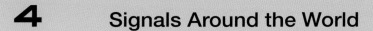

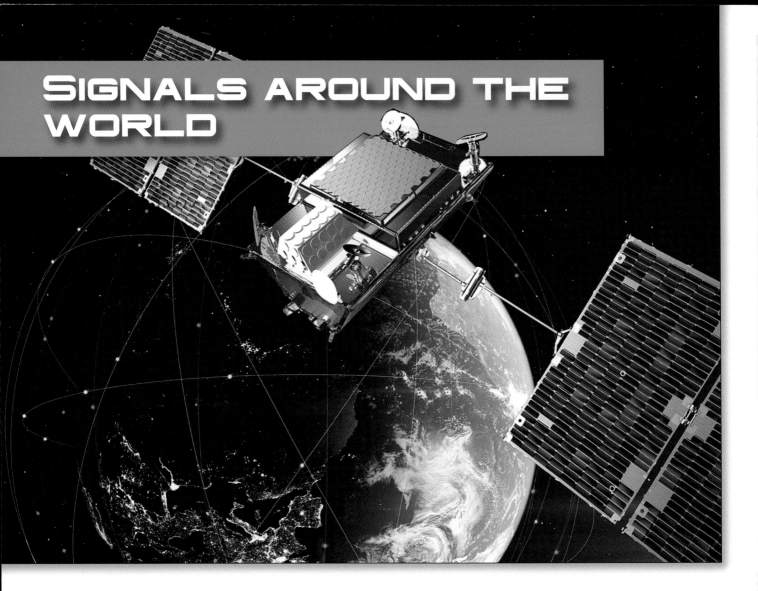

SIGNALS AROUND THE WORLD

Making, launching, and operating artificial satellites is the biggest money-maker in space.

↑ A communications satellite (comsat) orbits high above Earth.

→ How do satellites work?

A satellite doesn't work all by itself. After construction and inspection, a rocket is used to launch it into space. Once in **orbit**, the satellite sends and receives electronic signals to and from one or more ground stations.

← A rocket roars off a launch pad, on its way to placing a satellite into space.

→ How high does a satellite fly?

Depending on the type of satellite, its operating height may be from a minimum of 100 miles (160 km) above Earth, to as high as 22,000 miles (36,000 km).

← Ground stations receive and send satellite data to billions of users around the world.

→ Why do satellites operate at different heights?

Satellites are built for many purposes. Earth observation satellites need to record precise detail for making maps or monitoring weather. This purpose is best served by operating in low Earth orbit (LEO), about 250 miles (400 km) above Earth.

At 22,000 miles (36,000 km) above Earth, a geostationary Earth orbit (GEO) satellite appears to stay in one position over the equator. This is useful for TV broadcasts because the satellite can reach much of the world at once. It also allows you to have a low-cost ground **antenna**, which you can attach to a wall or roof.

→ Will we use satellites on other planets?

In the future, local satellite networks will let space explorers and **colonists** communicate with each other, and use computer networks such as the Internet.

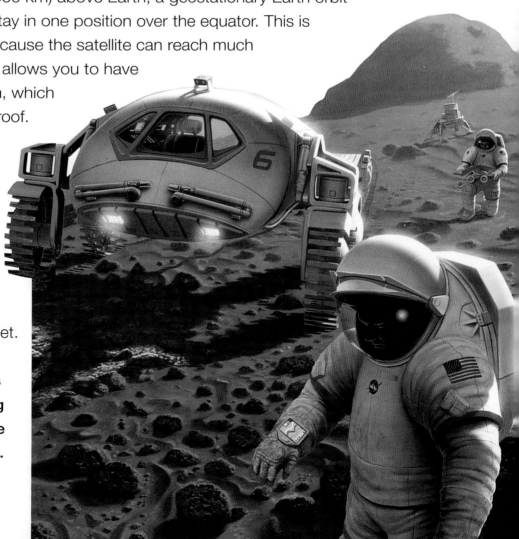

→ In this 2030s scene, Mars explorers stay in touch using nearby satellites. The vehicle has a rear-mounted antenna.

ASSEMBLING A SATELLITE

A satellite costs a huge amount of money to develop, but once it reaches space it may operate for many years.

SSL 1300 satellite

→ How many satellites are built?

Satellite builders design for the future. For example, the company Space Systems/Loral (SSL) built its first satellite in 1960. Since then, SSL has built more than 250 satellites. The SSL 1300 has a successful basic design, which will be developed for many years to come.

→ Final checks on this SSL satellite include making sure that all components work perfectly, as it is designed to operate for years after leaving Earth.

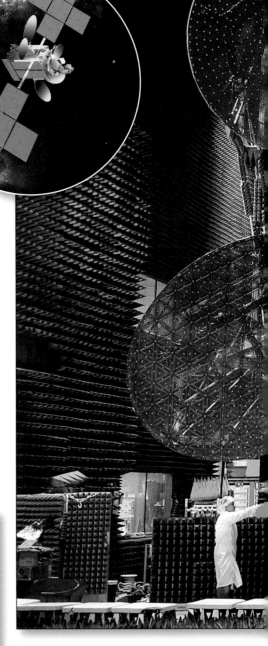

← Assembling a satellite means working in a **clean room**. Surgical gloves and a hair net are essential gear.

→ Who launches satellites once they are built?

International competition is stiff, even though it may cost $70-120 million for a large satellite launch. Companies from the US, Europe, and Russia offer their services, as do those of China, India, and Japan. American newcomer SpaceX aims to beat them all on price, offering cheaper launches with its Falcon 9 rocket.

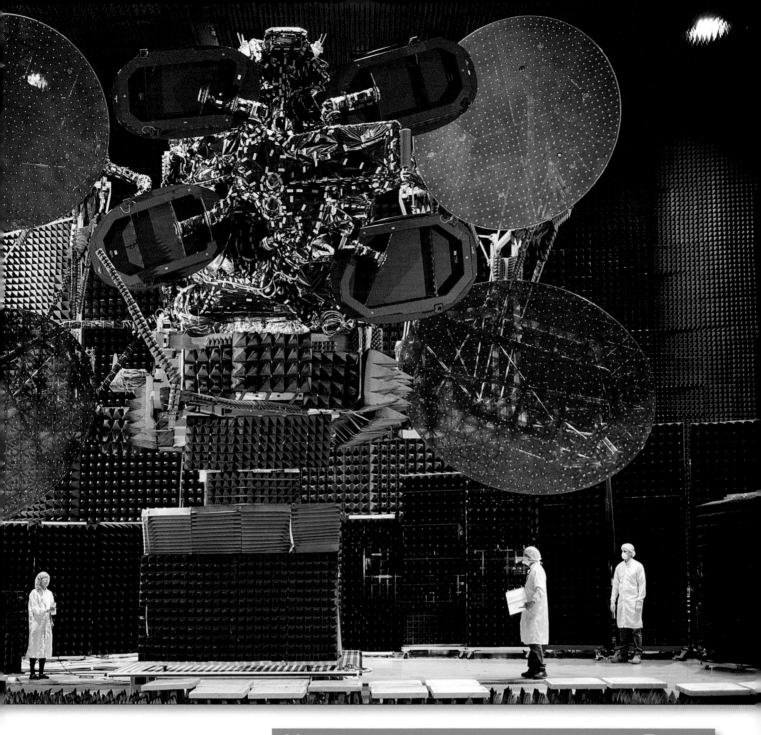

➜ Is there a traffic jam in space?

As you read this, about 3500 satellites are circling Earth. That sounds like a lot, but there is a huge amount of empty space for them to move. Despite this, the danger of collision is steadily increasing each year.

HOW MUCH DOES A SATELLITE COST?

Precise costs depend on a satellite's size, type, and where its orbit lies. However, the below figures give a fair idea of cost. Satellites are big business!

1. Manufacture: $150 million
2. Launch: $120 million
3. Launch insurance: $20 million
4. Insurance in space: $20 million
5. Operating costs for about 15 years: $15 million

OBSERVING EARTH

Earth observation satellites, such as the Landsat series, supply information that helps us make the world a better—and safer—place.

Landsat 2 of 1975-82

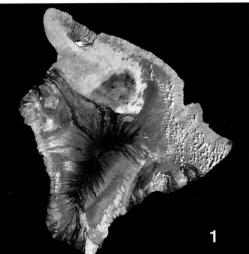

1

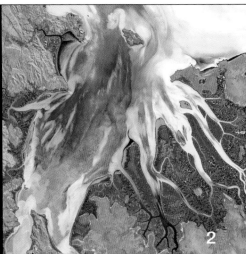

2

3

→ What is Landsat?

Landsat is the longest-running Earth observation satellite series. Landsat 1 was launched in 1972, while the latest Landsat 9 (below) is planned for service in 2020.

↑ **Landsat pictures include forests and volcanoes in Hawaii (1). Flowing water shows clearly in Australia (2), as does the circular Lake Manicouagan in the province of Quebec, Canada (3).**

Equipment "bus" carries Landsat's electronics

Solar panels change the energy in sunlight into electricity to power the onboard systems

→ What do Landsat sensors study?

They report on pollution, temperature, ground movements, crop yields, and diseases. They can also view changes on Earth, such as retreating glaciers and the shrinking Aral Sea.

⬇ Landsat pictures show fire (bright red), burned land (dark red) and smoke at Fort McMurray, Canada (4). Alaskan rivers are color coded. The lighter the color, the faster the water is moving (5). Green circles mark an irrigation scheme in Saudi Arabia (6).

➜ How do I access Landsat information?
Users used to be charged a fee for data, but today, Landsat data can be accessed online for free.

➜ Are there other satellites like Landsat?
At least 20 countries run their own Earth observation programs, and the data supplied saves time, money, and lives. Monitoring pollution is important, too. For example, the European **Envisat** kept a careful sky-spy watch on a big oil spill off the coast of Spain in 2002.

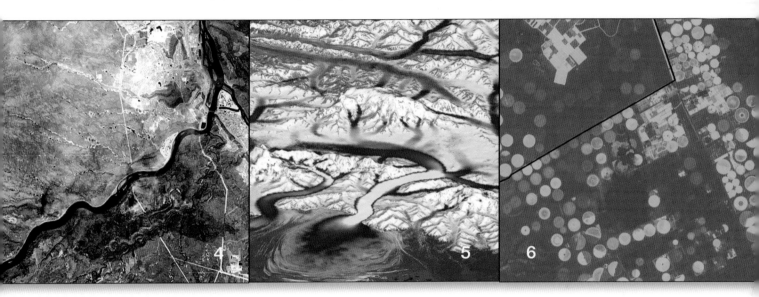

➜ What about the future?
Improved flows of data from satellite **sensors** will help us use our world's resources efficiently. With Earth's population increasing, we need data to understand how best to meet people's basic needs, while also doing less damage to the environment. Data can also help us warn people of imminent natural disasters, such as an earthquake or **tsunami**.

⬇ GRACE-FO is a two-unit system that will measure water levels and movements. Communities will use the data to understand the human impact on water where they live.

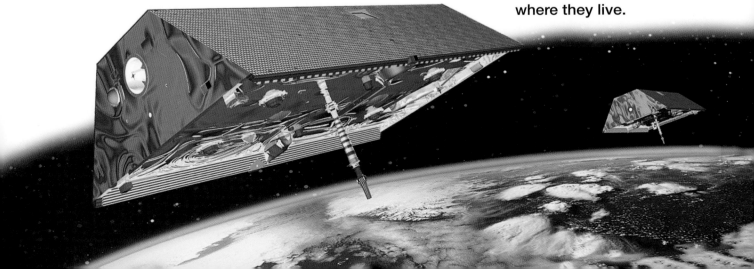

FINDING THE WAY

Satellite navigation (satnav) has transformed how we travel from place to place. Its accuracy means that few people now depend on paper maps.

Mobile devices use satnav information

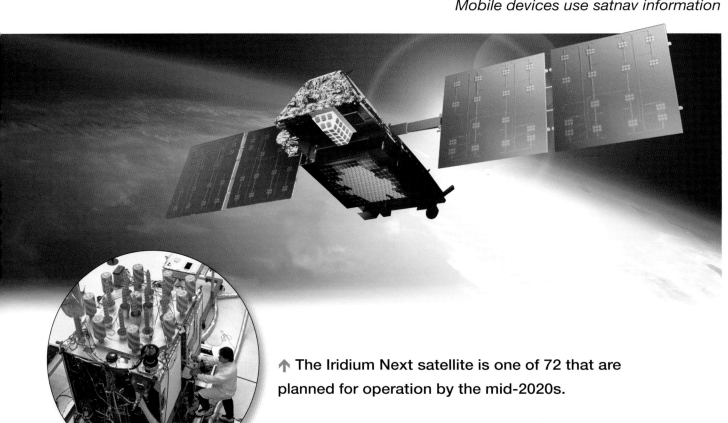

↑ The Iridium Next satellite is one of 72 that are planned for operation by the mid-2020s.

↑ The antennas of this GPS satellite are being checked before the craft is passed as fit for service. Next stop will be a launch to orbit for a multi-year satnav mission.

→ What is GPS?

GPS stands for Global Positioning System. It consists of more than 30 satellites, all run by the US government. Each satellite sends out a radio signal, which mobile device users can use to determine their position to within 16 feet (5 m).

→ What is the Iridium constellation?

The US communications company Iridium calls its fleet of satellites a **constellation**, a term widely used in the space industry. Iridium sells data and phone services to many users, from large corporations to individuals.

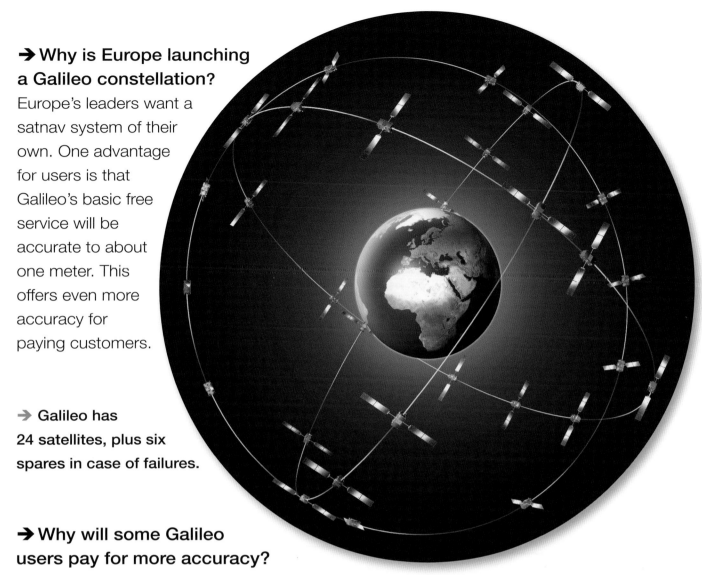

→ Why is Europe launching a Galileo constellation?

Europe's leaders want a satnav system of their own. One advantage for users is that Galileo's basic free service will be accurate to about one meter. This offers even more accuracy for paying customers.

→ Galileo has 24 satellites, plus six spares in case of failures.

→ Why will some Galileo users pay for more accuracy?

There are plenty of people who need it. For example, if you are a near-future farmer ready to buy a **robotic** tractor, accurate satnav data will be a core technology for it to work in the fields. And that will also be true for the self-driving cars and trucks of the 2020s.

← The Galileo constellation is planned for full operation after 2020. Control centers will be based in Germany and Italy.

WHAT DO YOU THINK?

Do you use a cell phone to find directions to a destination? If so, the route details will use satnav, most likely GPS. Can you think of any reasons that satnav might not be the best option to help you get around? Are traditional paper maps still useful?

THE ROCKETEERS

The way of the future is to stop using rockets designed for only one use. Several new rocket designs have proved that they can be reused again and again.

The European Ariane 6 launcher will fly in 2020

→ **Why stop using throwaway rocket launchers?**

The space race has been a story of improving rocket hardware, while developing more efficient computer software for guidance. Traditionally, rocket hardware has been thrown away during each launch, so the cost was always huge.

Things changed in December 2015, when the SpaceX company safely landed its Falcon 9 rocket after a launch.

↑ **The Blue Origin company has also launched and landed rockets successfully. This New Shepard model is designed to carry space tourists on short flights.**

→ What is a propulsive landing?

It describes being able to restart an engine during return to Earth, then using it as a braking method to make a controlled landing. This way, rockets won't simply fall back to Earth.

The SpaceX Falcon 9 was the first rocket to make a propulsive landing, though the test program had taken four years, with many crashes during that time.

← A Falcon 9 returning to Earth, a few seconds before landing. Moments before touchdown, four legs extend to keep the Falcon 9 upright after the engine shuts down.

→ Will all future rockets be reusable?

SpaceX and Blue Origin both plan to make reusability standard. But long-established launch companies, such as Arianespace from Europe, believe their throwaway launchers are reliable enough to remain competitive for many customers.

Even so, by the mid-2020s, later versions of the Ariane 6 will almost certainly be at least partly reusable.

WHY IS REUSABILITY IMPORTANT?

It mostly comes down to cost. Elon Musk of SpaceX compares reusable rockets to airplanes. Musk notes that if an airplane was thrown away after each flight, the huge cost would make air trips unaffordable for almost everyone.

AEROSPACE MACHINES

Rockets roaring off a launch pad are being joined by new launchers—some looking much like futuristic aircraft.

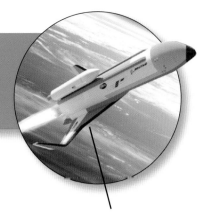

The Boeing Phantom Express will take off vertically, but land on a runway like an airplane

→ Are launchers with wings, or carrier planes, better than rockets?

For small and medium-sized satellites, a carrier plane can be cheaper than using a rocket to blast off a traditional launch pad. The carrier plane can be flown much like an airplane, but it carries a rocket instead of people. The rocket is dropped at high altitude, when it fires its own motor to fly on into space.

↑ The six-jet Stratolaunch carrier plane was designed to carry a rocket and satellite load under the huge wing.

→ Why is it cheaper to use a carrier plane?

Carrier planes are cheaper because they can be reused, replacing expensive throwaway launchers. The cost per flight needs to cover only aircraft maintenance, fuel, and pay for the air and ground crews.

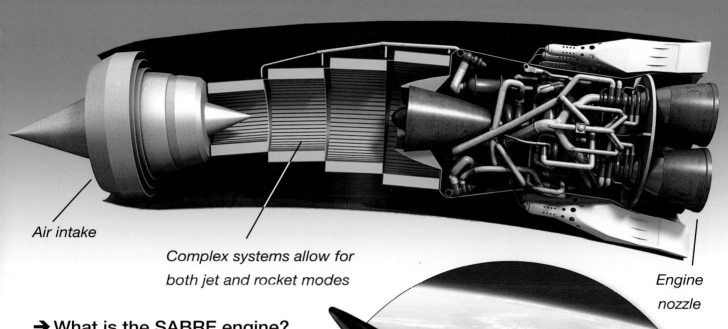

Air intake

Complex systems allow for
both jet and rocket modes

Engine
nozzle

→ What is the SABRE engine?

It is a British design (above) being
developed to power a spaceplane of
the future, called Skylon. SABRE
combines two engines in one. It
uses jet mode to fly into the upper
atmosphere. Then, the engine
converts to rocket mode for higher
flight into space. On return from
orbit, SABRE turns back to jet mode,
to fly back to base. It lands smoothly
on a runway, like an airplane.

→ A SABRE engine on each wingtip could
power the Skylon spaceplane. Here, Skylon's load
bay doors are open, ready to release a science experiment.

→ What does SABRE mean?

SABRE stands for
Synergistic Air-Breathing
Rocket Engine. The engine
design is based on the work
of Alan Bond, a leading
aerospace engineer.

WHERE ARE SPACEPORTS BEING BUILT?

Several countries have plans for new spaceports, or places
where spacecraft are launched. One of these is a joint
venture between Canada and the Ukraine.

Maritime Launch Services (MLS) is building a spaceport in
Nova Scotia, from where Cyclone-4M rockets will take off.
Nova Scotia is enthusiastic about the spaceport because it
is a private venture, so no provincial funding is needed. Also,
the spaceport could become a popular tourist destination.

JUNKYARD IN SPACE

Space debris is already a serious issue. More flights in the future could increase the chance of collisions between spacecraft and pieces of debris. Some scientists are working on solving the problem with orbital garbage collectors.

→ Where does space debris come from?
Bigger pieces of debris can be from used rocket boosters, or discarded satellite casings. Smaller items range from nuts, bolts, and screws to stray flecks of paint.

↑ A future clean-up spacecraft carefully approaches the drifting debris of a space collision.

→ **Computers track nearly 20,000 pieces of space waste. There are millions more that are far too small to follow.**

→ Have there been any major collisions?
None so far have endangered astronauts, but at least five satellites have collided with debris, including a craft from the Iridium constellation. The **International Space Station** (ISS) sometimes moves itself out of harm's way by adjusting its orbit. But in 2016, astronaut Tim Peake noted that it has a cracked window—likely from a collision.

➜ Can we tackle space junk?

Loading several satellites on a rocket reduces the number of spent casings to dispose of, and can also lower the cost of a launch. But new types of small satellites may create more problems. They will be launched in large numbers, and keeping track of them all may prove difficult, or impossible.

⬆ In the 2030s, aerospace craft similar to this American SR-72 concept may launch special clean-up craft into space.

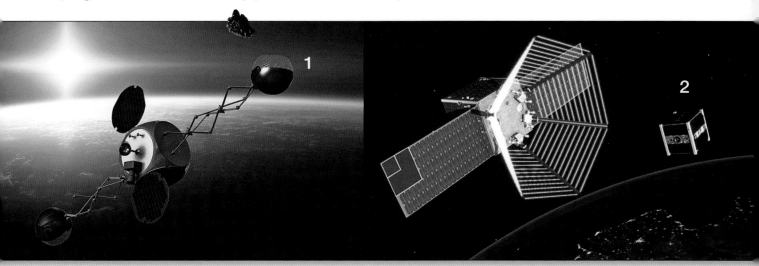

⬆ Two future spacecraft that may help clear space debris. The Slingsat (1) unfolds arms that scoop up chunks of drifting material. This six-sided space garbage collector could remove the fridge-sized Cubesat (2) from orbit.

CANADA TO THE RESCUE?

The company MDA from Canada makes the **Canadarm2** and **Dextre** repair **robot**, used on the ISS. Now MDA is working on a refuelling and servicing spacecraft. When built, it could reduce the need for new satellites, by keeping existing ones in service longer.

MADE IN SPACE

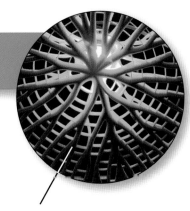

3D printing will allow space companies to manufacture items in space that are cheaper and more effective than those made on Earth.

Complex shapes are easily made with a 3D printer

→ What is 3D printing?

3D printers create objects by adding thin layers of material, ending up with a precisely shaped object. Experiments on the International Space Station have shown that 3D printing is highly suited for use in space.

↑ **The Made in Space company tested 3D printing in this special aircraft. After that, the printer was used successfully aboard the ISS.**

→ What is the advantage of 3D printing?

3D printers are lightweight and they do not create waste. Instructions can come remotely from a computer program. To date, small tools have been made using 3D printing on the ISS. In the future, printing out complex items, such as robotic devices, may be possible.

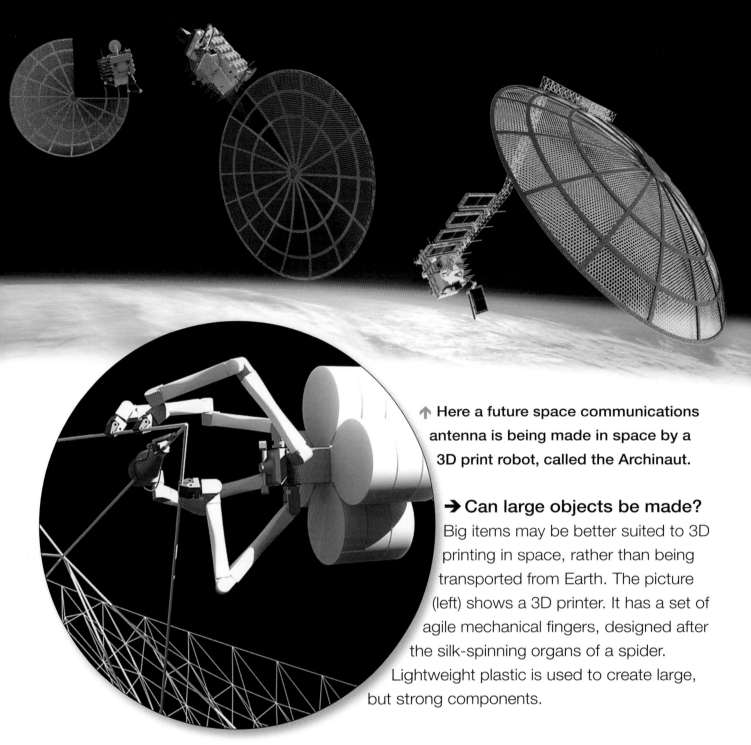

↑ Here a future space communications antenna is being made in space by a 3D print robot, called the Archinaut.

→ Can large objects be made?

Big items may be better suited to 3D printing in space, rather than being transported from Earth. The picture (left) shows a 3D printer. It has a set of agile mechanical fingers, designed after the silk-spinning organs of a spider. Lightweight plastic is used to create large, but strong components.

→ Could a 3D printer make an entire spacecraft?

3D printing technology is already being used widely. For example, the SpaceX rocket company has tested 3D parts for its powerful SuperDraco engine. One day, a 3D printer could create a spacecraft.

DO YOU WISH TO GO SPACE CAMPING?

Jason Dunn, of Made In Space, says that "...space exploration is a lot like a camping trip. If something goes wrong or there's an emergency, you've got to go home to fix it." Things could be made much easier if spacecraft carry their own 3D printer, with raw materials to make a whole range of spare parts. Dunn adds, "3D printing will allow independence from Earth."

SPACE SUITS

A suit is worn to work in space. As we further our space activity, new suit designs will be needed. Different space suits will be used in spacecraft, for space walks, or for exploring other worlds.

Space suit for space walks, used by US Shuttle astronauts

→ What is the Boeing Blue space suit?

This has been designed for astronauts to wear inside the Boeing Starliner spacecraft. It is a suit worn inside a spacecraft, that will keep crew alive in case anything goes wrong.

↑ **The Boeing Blue suit being tested in a Starliner. The suit is lighter and cooler than previous types.**

→ Could I spacewalk in the Boeing Blue suit?

Not really. The Boeing Blue does not have the equipment needed to keep an astronaut alive for the several hours taken for a typical space walk. It has no onboard maneuvering thrusters either, so cannot be used to move around outside.

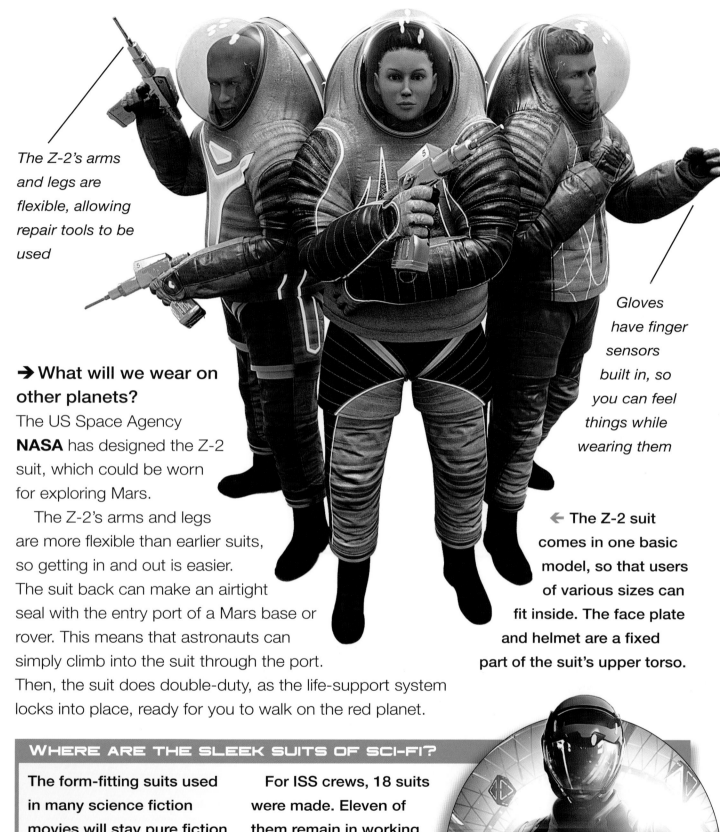

The Z-2's arms and legs are flexible, allowing repair tools to be used

Gloves have finger sensors built in, so you can feel things while wearing them

→ **What will we wear on other planets?**

The US Space Agency **NASA** has designed the Z-2 suit, which could be worn for exploring Mars.

The Z-2's arms and legs are more flexible than earlier suits, so getting in and out is easier. The suit back can make an airtight seal with the entry port of a Mars base or rover. This means that astronauts can simply climb into the suit through the port. Then, the suit does double-duty, as the life-support system locks into place, ready for you to walk on the red planet.

← **The Z-2 suit comes in one basic model, so that users of various sizes can fit inside. The face plate and helmet are a fixed part of the suit's upper torso.**

WHERE ARE THE SLEEK SUITS OF SCI-FI?

The form-fitting suits used in many science fiction movies will stay pure fiction for the time being. The technology needed to create these suits lies at least a decade or two ahead.

For ISS crews, 18 suits were made. Eleven of them remain in working condition. Improved suits built for future space walks will not be perfected until the mid-2020s.

ROBOTS AT THE READY

BY 2030, robots will be used for many tasks aboard spacecraft. They will be especially useful as assistants during space walks.

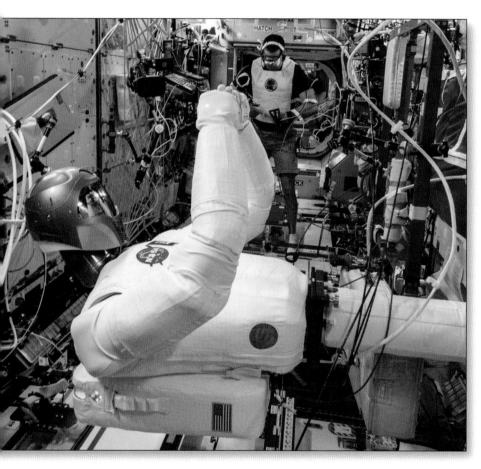

← Robonaut is seen here in the ISS, during manipulator tests. The experimental program will eventually mean that humans and robots can work together.

→ What is the NASA Robonaut?

Robonaut has been ongoing aboard the ISS since 2012. The first Robonaut (R1) had manipulator hands that could work much like those of a human.

→ What about Robonaut2?

R2 took the project further, by adding a pair of legs, faster software, and hardware upgrades. The human-like design of R2 allows it to develop its range of abilities beside ISS astronauts.

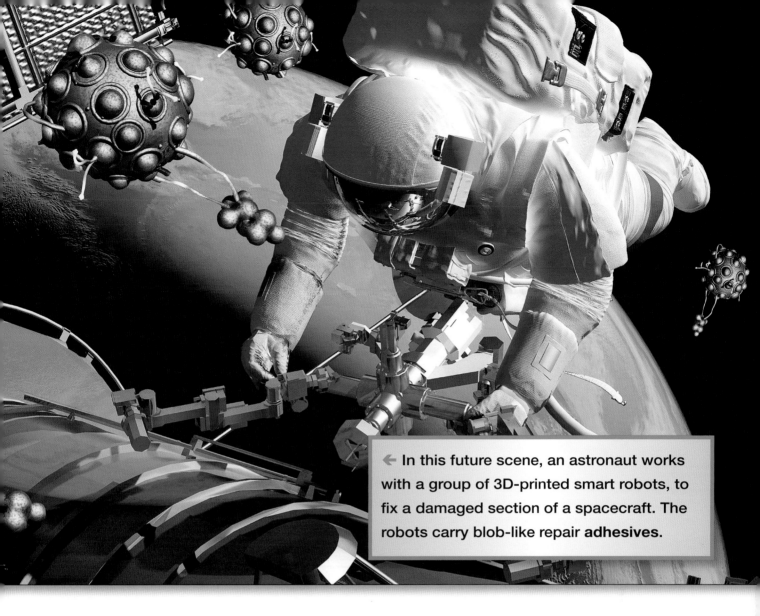

← In this future scene, an astronaut works with a group of 3D-printed smart robots, to fix a damaged section of a spacecraft. The robots carry blob-like repair **adhesives**.

→ How will robots work in spaceships of the future?

Robots will perform routine equipment inspections, and help with maintenance work. They will also help astronauts by performing more difficult tasks during space walks, and eventually may take over much—or even all—dangerous work outside a spacecraft.

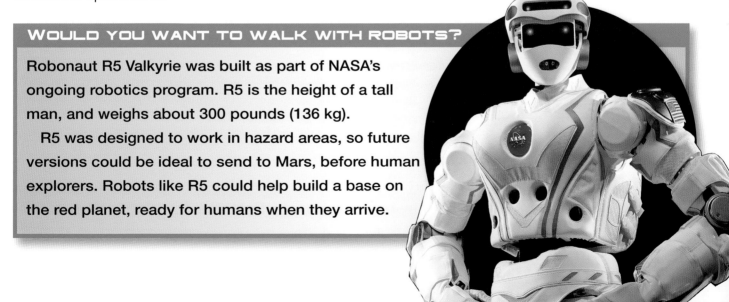

WOULD YOU WANT TO WALK WITH ROBOTS?

Robonaut R5 Valkyrie was built as part of NASA's ongoing robotics program. R5 is the height of a tall man, and weighs about 300 pounds (136 kg).

R5 was designed to work in hazard areas, so future versions could be ideal to send to Mars, before human explorers. Robots like R5 could help build a base on the red planet, ready for humans when they arrive.

SPACE MEDICINE

Space is a deadly environment, though research shows that some of its dangers may be reduced in the future.

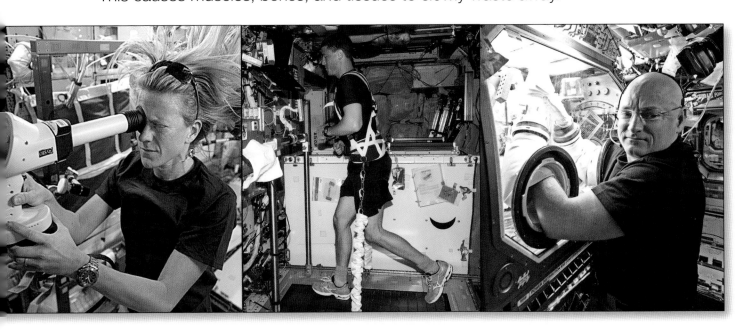

ISS crews carry out a large amount of medical research

→ Why is space so dangerous?

The obvious dangers to astronauts include the space environment itself, where there is nothing to eat, drink, or breathe. Crews of the International Space Station need regular supplies, sent up from Earth by various cargo spacecraft. But living in the gravity-free ISS for long periods means that astronauts cannot exercise their bodies as we do on Earth. This causes muscles, bones, and tissues to slowly waste away.

→ How do astronauts stay healthy in space?

Regular exercising with the ISS treadmill helps to provide a partial solution. However, astronauts have to use a special harness to hold them down to the running track, otherwise they would simply float away after a few seconds.

↑ Science activities keep ISS crews busy during their months-long stays on board.

→ What happens when astronauts return to Earth?

They are usually extremely weak at first, but their muscles recover after a few weeks.

⬆ This concept shows a possible future medical research base, in orbit above Earth. There, scientists could continue with work presently done in the ISS.

➔ Are there any health solutions for future space travelers?

Future spacecraft could include a rotating section inside, called a centrifuge. This gives a sensation of gravity, and by visiting the section regularly, astronauts could reduce muscle and bone loss.

More medical research is needed, both in the ISS and at future research facilities, such as the orbiting medical station shown above.

RESEARCH ABOVE EARTH

The ISS is a space home for many research programs, including methods of reducing bone weakening. Other work includes studies for asthma treatment, new vaccines, and anti-cancer drugs. There is also work to help create advanced medical robots, and improved disease treatments.

MOON MINERS

The Moon is Earth's nearest neighbor in space. There are resources we can benefit from there, if we can find a way to access them.

→ Why return to the Moon?

The last human on the Moon was US astronaut Eugene Cernan, of the 1972 **Apollo 17** mission. But now, improved technology has combined with international competition, from countries like China and India. So in the future, Earth's natural satellite will become a stage where countries and companies can demonstrate their advanced technology.

↑ The Shackleton Energy Company has plans for water-seeking lunar prospectors. Water on the Moon could be found, frozen as ice, in shadowed craters near the Moon's polar regions.

↑ A large base like this is still a future dream. However, lunar resources could allow a habitat like this to survive without needing supplies brought from Earth.

→ Why is the Moon useful?

Though far smaller than Earth, the Moon has plenty of land area—slightly less than that of Asia. National space agencies and commercial companies are all interested to see what they can find there. For example, if hydrogen could be mined in an affordable way, it can be used as fuel for spacecraft to explore the whole **Solar System**.

→ Why use the Moon as a base for future space missions?

The Moon's gravity is just one-sixth of Earth, which means that launching spacecraft from the Moon is much easier and cheaper. A rocket doesn't need as much fuel to leave the Moon. Calculations indicate that it could be 50-60 times cheaper to run a Moon flight business than doing it from Earth.

A future Moon mine, with tanks to store helium 3

→ Could I work on the Moon?

Being a Moon miner might be a late-21st century version of digging for gold in 1850s California. But working on the Moon will be dangerous, especially if vital equipment should fail.

FUTURE FUEL?

Chinese scientists aim to see if there are large amounts of helium 3 on the Moon. The gas could be used as a low-pollution fuel in new types of power stations, here on Earth.

UNLIMITED FUTURE?

Eventually, we could mine raw materials from objects across the entire Solar System. As well as the Moon and planets, there are countless **asteroids**, which might supply resources one day.

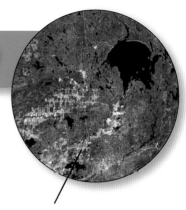

In Canada, nickel has been mined from the remains of an ancient meteor

→ Where will we find resources?
The first steps in space mining are already underway, with a company such as Planetary Resources, which aims to survey likely asteroids. Deep Space Industries (DSI) has similar aims, and plans to start processing an asteroid as soon as the 2020s.

↑ A DSI Dragonfly probe settles on the rocky surface of an asteroid. It will take samples to see if there are valuable materials there.

→ Isn't it easier to mine materials here on Earth?
We have been mining our world for centuries. But creating a non-polluting future means doing things differently, and perhaps that means mining in space.

➔ How much is out there?

If estimates are correct, there is no real limit to what we can find in space. A single, medium-size asteroid could provide metals such as nickel, iron, or cobalt. Hydrogen, oxygen, and ammonia are also common on space objects, as are ices containing water.

COULD YOU WORK AWAY FROM EARTH?

Right now, the way to join in the new space race is to work with a pioneer resources company.

In the decades to come, humans and robots could work together in opening up the riches of the Solar System. However, these jobs might be lonely, as even nearby asteroids are not in Earth's orbit. Mining the asteroids between Mars and Jupiter could mean being in deep space for months, or even years, at a time.

⬆ This future scene shows a mining base in the far-off asteroid belt, between the planets Mars and Jupiter.

➔ Will we build factories in space?

Eventually, many industries may be moved away from Earth. They could be built in space, to preserve our planet's environment. This idea may seem like an impossible dream, but some see it as a real possibility. Jeff Bezos, head of online retail giant Amazon, once suggested if all heavy industries could be moved to space, Earth could become a park for us all to enjoy.

GLOSSARY

3D printing Term for additive technology, in which thin layers of material are added until they build up to form a three-dimensional object. The 3D printer takes instructions from a computer program.

adhesives Substances used to stick objects or materials together

antenna Any piece of equipment that broadcasts or receives data from an electronic source. May be dish-or rod-shaped.

Apollo 17 The last of six crewed US Moon landing missions, flown in December, 1972

asteroid Rocky or metallic chunk of space debris, drifting in the Solar System

artificial satellite Spacecraft that orbits another space object, such as a planet or moon. More than 3500 are currently in orbit around Earth, though many are no longer in working condition.

↑ Robonaut R2 aboard the ISS, in 2014.

Canadarm2, Dextre Used on the ISS, both are manipulator devices. For example, Canadarm2 (*see the picture on page 1*) can attach to an approaching spacecraft, then bring it close, to lock safely onto the ISS.

clean room Term for a controlled environment with little or no dust, stray particles, or pollutants

colonist Someone who populates or has control over an area

commerce The large-scale activity of buying and selling

constellation Term for group of satellites following the same orbit, such as Galileo and Iridium

data General term for electronic information

Envisat Environmental satellite, operated by the European Space Agency (ESA) from 2002-12

helium 3 A material thought to be more common on the Moon than on Earth. It could be a fuel for future power stations, and would create very little pollution.

International Space Station (ISS) A base that orbits Earth and holds a crew of up to six astronauts

NASA National Aeronautics and Space Administration, the US space agency formed in 1958

orbit A curving path through space by one object around a bigger one. Artificial satellites circle Earth in three main orbital zones: Geostationary Earth orbit (GEO), Low Earth orbit

(LEO), and Medium Earth orbit (MEO).

robot, robotic A machine that can carry out complex instructions, with no human to operate it

sensor Mechanical device that is sensitive to light, temperature, sound, or many other factors. Transmits results to a measuring or control instrument.

Solar System The Sun and planets, plus moons, comets, asteroids, and other space matter

tsunami Unusually large sea wave, produced by an undersea earthquake or volcanic explosion

People mentioned in the book:

Bezos, Jeff (1964-) American chief of the online store, Amazon. Also head of the Blue Origin space company, which he founded in 2000.

Bond, Alan (1944-) British engineer who is working on various advanced projects. These include the Skylon spaceplane and SABRE engine.

Cernan, Eugene (1934-2017) Commander of the final Apollo mission to the Moon, and the last man to stand on its surface

Dunn, Jason Co-founded the Made in Space 3D printing company, in 2010. Made in Space operates a 3D printer on the ISS, and works with

NASA on the Archinaut robotics program.

Musk, Elon (1971-) South African-born, Canadian-American founder of the SpaceX rocket company, and other high-tech ventures

Peake, Tim (1972-) British Army Corps Officer and European Space Agency astronaut, who was a crew member on the ISS for just over 6 months in 2015 and 2016

WEBSITES

There is no shortage of space-related information on the Internet. These sites reflect some of this book's content, and should give you a good start for carrying out your own research.

www.asc-csa.gc.ca
Visit the Canadian Space Agency and see its plans

www.blueorigin.com
Information on rockets and space tourism

www.boeing.com/space/starliner
Details of the Starliner spacecraft and space suit

www.esa.int/ESA
Website of the European Space Agency

www.madeinspace.us
Information about the 3D printing company

www.nasa.gov
Website of the world's biggest space agency

www.spacex.com
Website of the pioneer space launch company

INDEX

ABOUT THE AUTHOR

David Jefferis has written more than 100 non-fiction books on science, technology, and futures.

His works include a seminal series called World of the Future, as well as more than 30 other science books for Crabtree Publishing.

David's merits include the London Times Educational Supplement Award, and also Best Science Books of the Year. Follow David online at: www.davidjefferis.com